Christian: Personally, this book was very fun to write because it's all about giving back and helping those in need. Not only is it the right thing to do, but it's also fun, and you can learn quite a bit. My dad and I hope you like the book and grow to love helping others. Enjoy!

Bill: Christian and I had a great time working on this book together. We have been inspired by the many acts of kindness we have seen, and have enjoyed helping out as a family along with our friends at Homewood Suites and Hilton Worldwide — the stories you read in this book have all happened thanks to our friends. Thanks for reading!

One Friday morning at Duck Inc., Mr. Wood walked into Lewis' office. "Lewis," he said, "we need your help. We've become very successful at Duck Inc., and it's time we gave back and helped others in our community." He continued, "I'd like your help.' "Great!" replied Lewis, excited at the prospect. "I'd be happy to help."

That night, Lewis told his wife, Lois, about his meeting with Mr. Wood. "Wow," she said excitedly, "that is quite an honor."

Lewis nodded his head and agreed. "I've been thinking about this for a while. I'm thankful for the nice things we have, like our beautiful home and the fun trips we get to take."

Their ducklings, Lance and Lisa, chimed in. "Especially the fun trips!"

ater, during family game night, Lisa told her parents that she wanted to help, too. "Don't forget to count me in," piped up Lance. "I want to help!"

Lois, feeling proud of her family, joined in, as well. Lewis was excited to hear that his family wanted to help. How would they get started?

n Monday, Lewis went into work with an idea.

He asked his coworkers if they had any, as well.

One duck said, "We could build a library for Duckling Elementary School and fill it with books."

Another duck quickly added, "...or we could help clean up the Duck River in Tennessee..."

"What about helping the homeless? We could collect food, water, and clothes," said another one.

"Wow, those are all great ideas," said Lewis.

L ewis told Mr. Wood about the ideas. "Those are fantastic!" he exclaimed. "Who says we can't do all three?"

Lewis went back to his team and shared the good news. "Mr. Wood liked all our suggestions and wants to try them all. Is everyone up for the challenge?"

"Of course!" exclaimed his coworkers together. The plan had begun.

"We can ask for help from our coworkers…"

"…and our families and friends, too…"

"Why don't we call your friends at Homewood Suites, and see if they would help?"

"Good ideas, everyone!" said Lewis excitedly. "I will call my friend, Jan, whom I met at the first Homewood Suites I stayed in; she's just moved here to Duckville."

"We'd love to help out," said Jan Smith, the hotel general manager. "The team here at the hotel will be glad to chip in." She addressed her team, "We need to help Lewis and his friends. Are you in with helping?"

"Yes!" they shouted.

A nd so they went to work. First, they went to Duckling Elementary and met with the school's principal, Mr. Sanchez. "We are so thankful for our new library, Lewis. I know the children will learn so much from all the new books."

The team went to work on the library. It was hard work, but they knew it was worth it.

The schoolchildren were delighted. There were so many books! To celebrate the library's opening, Lewis and his friends read to the children.

Next, the group went to work on cleaning up the Duck River.

"We're so glad you're here," said their guide, Tonya. "I'd like to share some neat facts about the Duck River."

DUCK RIVER

- 270 MILES LONG!
- OVER 150 SPECIES OF FISH
- 55 SPECIES OF MUSSELS
- CONSIDERED ONE OF THE MOST BIOLOGICALLY DIVERSE BODIES OF WATER IN NORTH AMERICA
- HOME TO MANY ANIMALS, INCLUDING DUCKS, BLUE HERON, MUSSELS, FISH, TURTLES, AND BEAVERS.

ewis, his family, and everyone from Homewood Suites hotels went to work on the riverbanks. They picked up garbage and debris that people had thrown out.

"Wow," thought Lewis, "this is hard work. I can see why you should only throw garbage in garbage cans!"

THANKS!

On their last volunteer project, the team set their sights on The Nest House, a local homeless shelter that helps families who do not have a home. Lewis and his team collected food and clothing at Duck Inc., while Homewood Suites hotels chipped in and donated soap, towels, sheets, and plenty of blankets.

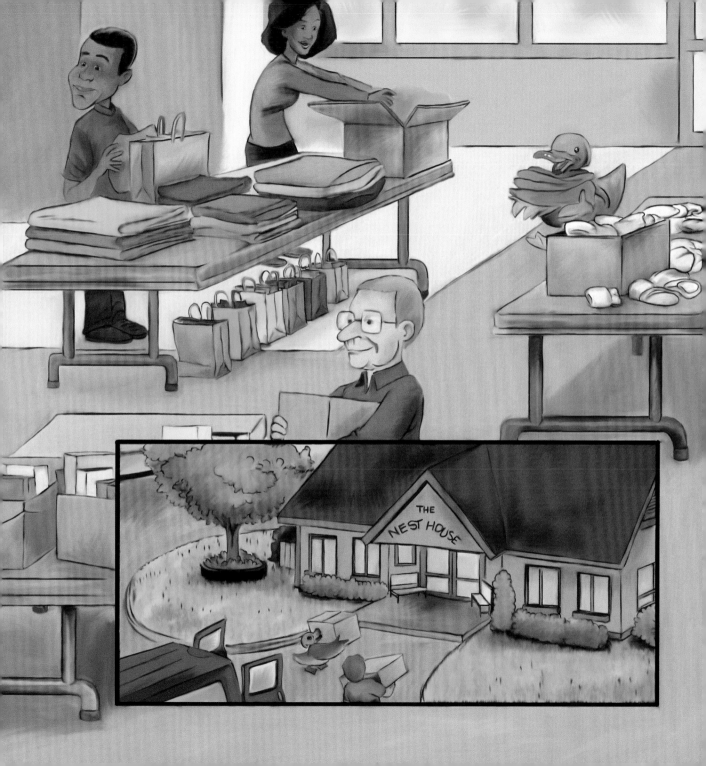

L ewis and the team sent the supplies to The Nest House. The shelter's manager, Mr. Jones, was so glad to have such much-needed supplies. "Lewis, you and your friends have helped many less fortunate than yourselves. We really appreciate what you've done."

The next day, Mr. Wood thanked Lewis, his friends, his family, and all the volunteers from Duck Inc. "I'm proud of you, your team, your friends at Homewood Suites, and your family. You've made us all proud, but most importantly, you've made our world a better place. You should all be proud of yourselves for helping so many."

That night, Lewis was tired, but pleased. As he sat in his favorite chair, he thought about other projects that could benefit his community. There was always more to do.

The Story of Lewis

Our guests often ask, "Why the duck?
Who is he and what does a duck have to do with Homewood Suites?"

Homewood Suites chose a duck because it symbolizes versatility and adaptability. Ducks are comfortable in air, in water, and on land. They migrate long distances over extended periods. And their ability to adapt and thrive in a variety of places represents our goal in the travel and hospitality industry – to serve guests with resourcefulness and flexibility.

We chose a wood duck, considered one of the most beautiful creatures in nature. And we've given him a name – Lewis. By naming Lewis and bringing him to life, we've created a visual representation of a unique brand that caters to those who want the comforts of home when on the road for a few days or more. And, with Lewis to guide us, there is no doubt that we will meet our guests' individual needs for comfort, flexibility and convenience.

HOMEWOOD
SUITES
BY HILTON®

Lewis also represents Homewood's desire to reach beyond our guests to the community around us through our **Nature**, **Nurture**, **Learn** principle.

NATURE. Once almost extinct, the wood duck population has survived partly due to the preservation of the woodland and wetland habitats. Protecting our natural surroundings is vital for our environment. Homewood partners with the Duck River in Tennessee and several other organizations in an effort to preserve earth's most valuable natural resources.

NURTURE. Just as ducks migrate to find a new, safe home, it is our goal to do our part to assist the homeless with finding safety and security. Through various sponsorships, Homewood Suites hotels focus on providing assistance for those who need a place to call home – a place where they can BE AT HOME.

LEARN. The wood duck's survival rate is often dependent on learning to spread its wings and fly. Homewood's *Lewis the Duck* book series and partnership with the Books for Kids Reading Libraries, as well as other childhood literacy organizations, all have a unified goal of opening a world of opportunity for early childhood literacy through a solid foundation of learning. For more information on Books for Kids, visit www.booksforkids.org.